NORBERT'S BIG DREAM

BY LORI DEGMAN ★ ILLUSTRATED BY MARCO BUCCI

Most pigs are satisfied just rolling in the mud,

or slurping slop,

or snoozing in the shade.

But not Norbert.

Norbert was a pig with a dream.

Since he was a wee piglet, Norbert dreamed of swimming the English Channel.

And, when he was big enough, he started training.
"Finally!" said Norbert.

So, while the other pigs rolled in the mud, Norbert practiced his flutter kick.

While they slurped slop, Norbert munched muscle-building foods.

And while they snoozed in the shade, Norbert did push-ups.

Day after day Norbert trained.

Night after night he dreamed ...

...until the day he knew he was ready.

"I'm off to swim the English Channel!"
Norbert told his friends.

They snickered.

"No pig has ever crossed the English Channel—not even in a boat!" they said.

"Then I'll be the first!" Norbert shouted.

Norbert squeezed into his
swim trunks and cap.

He snapped on his goggles
and flopped into his flippers.

He greased himself up
to keep out the cold.

"I'm ready," he said. "Which way to the English Channel?"

Unfortunately, this was something Norbert hadn't considered.

Is it behind the barn? Nope.

Over the hill? Nope.

Around the bend? No channel.

"How can I cross the English Channel if I can't even find it?"
Norbert sighed. Maybe his big dream was only a dream after all.

He wiped off the grease.

He unsnapped his goggles and
flopped out of his flippers.

He peeled off his swim cap and plodded back toward the farm.

"Wait . . . what's that?"
Norbert squealed!

He huffed and puffed and piggy-paddled as hard as he could.

"Hurrah! I crossed Norbert's Channel! I'm living the dream!"

Norbert raced back to the farm to share the great news.

"Thanks, everyone! I wish you could have been there to see it!"

After the celebrations, things went back to normal on the farm.

The pigs rolled in the mud.

They slurped slop.

They snoozed in the shade.

NORBERT'S
CHANNEL
✓

But not Norbert.

Norbert was a pig with a new dream.

To my students—past, present, and future—dream big!

Lori

★

This book is for ip-hone.

Marco

Sleeping Bear Press®
2395 South Huron Parkway, Suite 200
Ann Arbor, MI 48104
www.sleepingbearpress.com

Printed and bound in China.

10 9 8 7 6 5 4 3 2 1

Library of Congress Cataloging-in-Publication Data

Names: Degman, Lori, author. | Bucci, Marco, illustrator.
Title: Norbert's big dream / by Lori Degman ; illustrated by Marco Bucci.
Description: Ann Arbor, MI : Sleeping Bear Press, [2016] | Summary: Norbert
has always dreamed of swimming the English Channel, and though he trains
every day, he realizes he does not know where it is, but his pig friends
help him succeed in his swimming quest.
Identifiers: LCCN 2016007652 | ISBN 9781585369591
Subjects: | CYAC: Pigs—Fiction. | Swimming—Fiction. | Determination
(Personality trait)—Fiction.
Classification: LCC PZ7.7.D447 No 2016 | DDC [E]—dc23
LC record available at https://lccn.loc.gov/2016007652